JPIC Sp
Spinell: W9-AJS-111
Princess Pig

$19.99
ocn236143128
1st ed.   10/04/2010

Princess
PIG

Written by
Eileen Spinelli

Illustrated by
Tim Bowers

Alfred A. Knopf · New York

To the women in my Wednesday-morning book group
—E.S.

To my good friend Lee Woolery
—T.B.

THIS IS A BORZOI BOOK PUBLISHED BY ALFRED A. KNOPF • Text copyright © 2009 by Eileen Spinelli • Illustrations copyright © 2009 by Tim Bowers
• All rights reserved. Published in the United States by Alfred A. Knopf, an imprint of Random House Children's Books, a division of Random House, Inc., New York.
• Knopf, Borzoi Books, and the colophon are registered trademarks of Random House, Inc. • Visit us on the Web! www.randomhouse.com/kids • Educators and librarians, for a variety of
teaching tools, visit us at www.randomhouse.com/teachers • *Library of Congress Cataloging-in-Publication Data* • Spinelli, Eileen. • Princess Pig / Eileen Spinelli ; illustrated by Tim
Bowers. — 1st ed. • p. cm. • Summary: A pig believes that she is a princess and behaves accordingly, but soon learns that being a royal has a price. • ISBN 978-0-375-84571-0 (trade) —
ISBN 978-0-375-94571-7 (lib. bdg.) • [1. Princesses—Fiction. 2. Pigs—Fiction. 3. Domestic animals—Fiction. 4. Contentment—Fiction. 5. Farm life—Fiction.] I. Bowers, Tim, ill. II. Title.
PZ7.S7566Pri 2009   [E]—dc22   2008024527 • The illustrations in this book were created using colored pencil and watercolor. • MANUFACTURED IN CHINA • June 2009
• 10 9 8 7 6 5 4 3 2 1 • First Edition • Random House Children's Books supports the First Amendment and celebrates the right to read.

One windy day—during the Picawash County Farm Show Parade—a peculiar thing happened. . . .

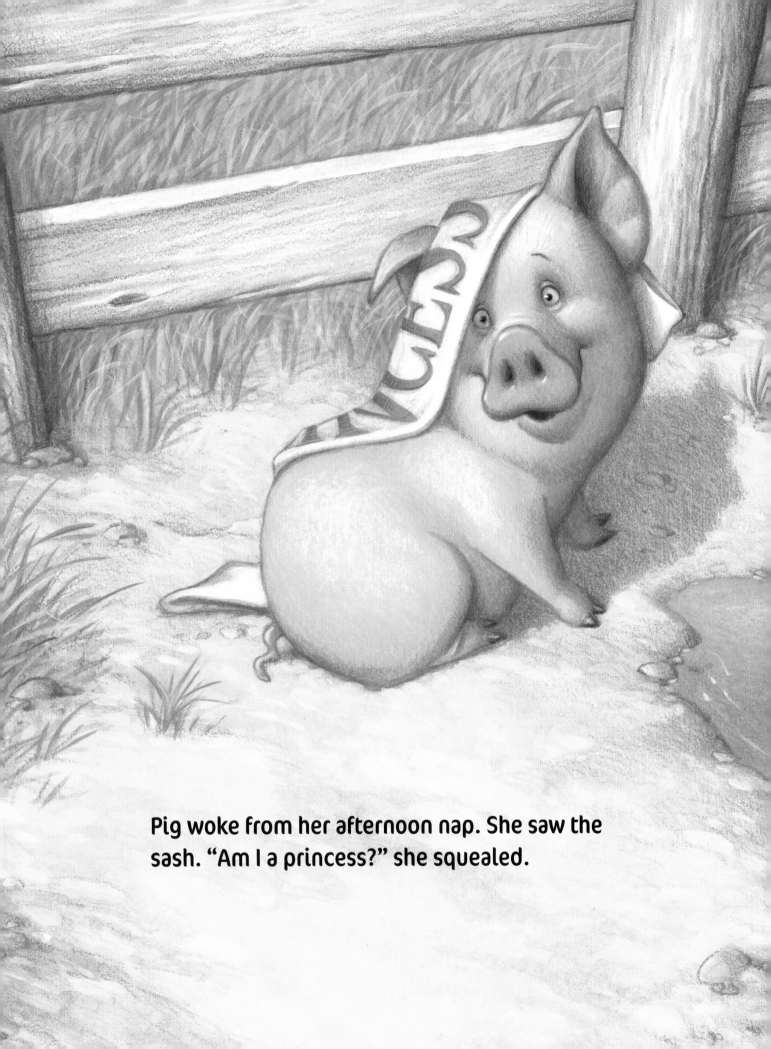

Pig woke from her afternoon nap. She saw the sash. "Am I a princess?" she squealed.

Goat shook his head. "You can't be a princess.
A princess wears a crown."

So Pig made herself a crown.
"Now I am a princess," declared Pig.

"You can't be a princess," said Cow. "You don't have a gold necklace."

So Pig wove a necklace that sparkled in the sunlight. Just like gold.
"I *am* a princess," insisted Pig.

"You can't be a princess," said Rooster, sniffing. "You don't smell like a princess."

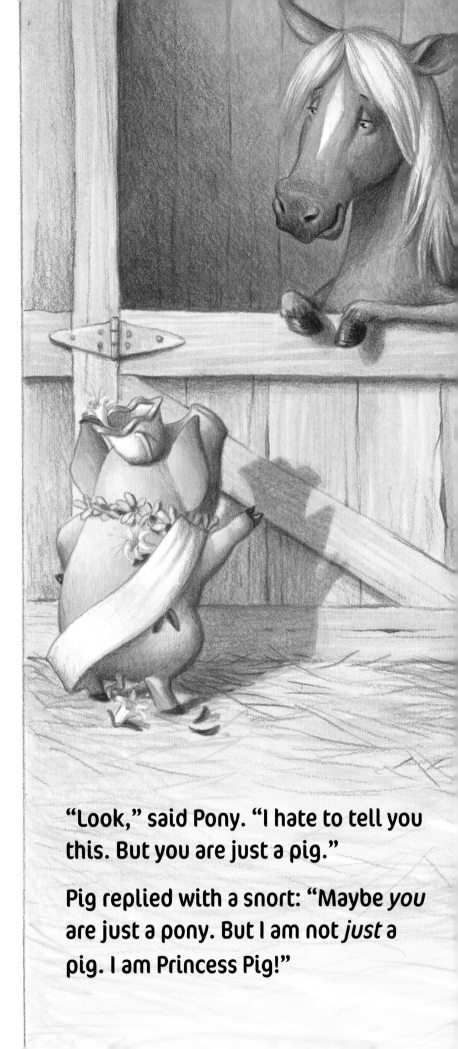

So Pig rolled herself in honeysuckle.
"I *am* a princess!" cried Pig.

"Look," said Pony. "I hate to tell you this. But you are just a pig."

Pig replied with a snort: "Maybe *you* are just a pony. But I am not *just* a pig. I am Princess Pig!"

Then Pig sat on the old tractor. "You can come visit with me as I sit on my royal throne."

"Wow!" said Goat. "I guess Pig *is* a princess."

"Sure looks like it," said Cow.

"Guess so," said Rooster.

"Nope," said Pony.

Soon the farmhand came with the slop can. "C'mon, piggy, piggy, pig!"

"No slop for me," said Pig. "*I* will have that pretty princess pie cooling on the windowsill."

Princess Pig got princess pie all over herself. And so after supper she declared: "The princess wishes to take a bath." Goat filled the tin tub with water.

"Very nice, Goat," Pig sniffed. "But where are my royal bubbles?"

"Oops," said Goat. "I'll be right back."

Soon Pig was basking in bubbles. "Ahhh . . .
I just love being a princess."

At bedtime Pig said to Cow: "I wish for a pillow soft enough for a princess." Cow brought back a sack of clean, fresh hay.

"Thank you. A lullaby'd go nice with this comfy pillow."

Cow and Rooster sang a lovely duet: "Moo-moo-cock-a-doodle-dooooooooo."

Pig yawned. "Enough. Now I'm ready to go to sleep. I wish for quiet, please."

"Your wish is our command," said Cow. "Good night, Princess Pig."

"Sweet dreams, Princess Pig," said Goat.

"Sleep tight, Princess Pig," said Rooster.

"Don't let the bedbugs bite," said Pony.

"Ha!" Pig snorted. "Bedbugs don't bite princesses."

"Maybe," said Pony. "But *you* are *not* a princess."

The very next morning, word got around that there was a princess living on the farm. Visitors started to come. Lots of visitors.

That very same morning, Pig wanted to sleep late.

"You can't sleep late," said Rooster.

"But I am a princess. I can sleep as late as I wish."

"Not today," said Rooster. "Da Vinci Duck is coming to paint your portrait."

Pig sighed. She put on her sparkly crown and her gold necklace. She posed in the hot sun while Da Vinci Duck painted . . . and painted . . . and painted.

When Duck finally finished, Cow hung the royal portrait in the barn.

Pig looked longingly at the cool mud in her pen. "I think I'll roll in the mud now—just a bit."

Goat was aghast. "Princesses *don't* roll in mud."

"They don't?"

"Nope," said Cow. "Let's see. . . . I know, you can roll in the herb garden. I think that will still be princessy."

But the herb garden
wasn't cool.
    Or squishy.
        Or soft.

And when evening came,
Pig found herself alone.

Pig went looking for the other animals.
There were lights on in the barn. She heard music and laughter.
Pig peeked through the door. "What's this?" she asked.

"Oh, it's just a regular old party," said Goat.

"A *great* regular old party!" said Pony.

Pig sniffled. "Why wasn't I invited?"

Cow bowed to Pig. "Because you are a princess. And I am just a cow. I don't live in a palace."

"Oh, of course. I understand." As she turned to leave, Pig wiped away a tear. "Well then . . . I'll say good night."

"Wait!" called Pony. "Why don't you stay?"

"I can't," explained Pig. "I am a *princess.*"

Pony rolled his eyes. "Pig, I'm going to say this one last time—you are NOT a princess."

Pig pondered. "I am . . . not?"

"No. You . . . are . . . a . . . pig. Just a regular old pig."

Pig stared at her royal portrait. "You know," she said, "that looks like me, but it's not, well, who I am."

"It's a fine thing to be a pig," said Pony. "If a pig is what you are."

Pig grinned. "You are one smart, regular old pony!"

Pig draped her sash over Rooster. She popped her crown
on Goat's head. She clasped her gold necklace around
Cow's neck.

"Three cheers for my loyal-royal friends!" cried Pig. And she headed to the good old dance floor with regular old Pony.